Three Grimms' Fairy Tales

Three
Grimms' Fairy Tales

Paintings by Gerard Wagner

Edited by Peter Stebbing

SteinerBooks 2012

This edition has been made possible with the support of private donations.

Published by SteinerBooks
610 Main Street, Great Barrington, Massachusetts 01230
www.steinerbooks.org

ISBN 978-0-88010-716-7

Library of Congress cataloging-in-publication data is available.

Cover Motif painted by Gerard Wagner for Briar Rose
Title Lettering: Peter Stebbing

Typesetting in Palatino: Urs Rüd, Basel

Three fairy tales collected by Jacob & Wilhelm Grimm. English text based
on the translation from the German by Jack Zipes.

Printed in China

CONTENTS

THE STAR-TALER

I.

THERE was once a little girl whose father and mother had died, and she was so poor that she no longer had a room in which to live nor a bed in which to sleep. In the end, she had nothing more than the clothes on her back and a little piece of bread in her hand that some kind soul had given her. To be sure, she was good and pious, and since she had been forsaken by the entire world, she went out into the countryside, trusting that the good Lord would look after her.

There she met a poor man, who said, "Ah, give me something to eat. I'm so hungry."
She handed him her entire piece of bread and said, "May God bless you," and continued on her way.

Then she encountered a child who moaned and said, "My head is cold. Give me something so I can cover it." The girl took off her cap and gave it to the child.

After she had gone a little way farther, she met another child, who had no jacket and was freezing. So she gave him hers.

And later on another child asked her for her little dress, and she gave it to her as well.

Finally, she reached a forest, and it had already become dark. Then another child came and asked for a little shirt, and the pious girl thought, It's dark, and nobody can see you. So you might as well give away your shirt. She took off the shirt and gave it away too.

And, as she stood there, with nothing on whatsoever, the stars fell from the sky all at once, and they turned into hard, shining taler coins. Though she had just given away her little shirt, she now had a new one of the finest linen. Thereupon, she gathered the coins together and was rich for the rest of her life.

BRIAR ROSE

II.

IN times of old there lived a king and queen, and every day they said, "Oh, if only we had a child!" Yet, they never had one.

Then one day, as the queen went out bathing, a frog happened to crawl ashore and say to her, "Your wish shall be fulfilled. Before the year is out, you shall give birth to a daughter."

The frog's prediction came true, and the queen gave birth to a girl who was so beautiful that the king was overjoyed and decided to hold a great feast. Not only did he invite his relatives, friends, and acquaintances, but also the wise women, in the hope that they would be generous and kind to his daughter. There were thirteen wise women in his kingdom, but he had only twelve golden plates from which they could eat. Therefore, one of them had to remain home.

The feast was celebrated with tremendous splendor, and when it drew to a close, the wise women bestowed their miraculous gifts upon the child. One gave her virtue, another beauty, the third wealth, and so on, until they had given her nearly everything one could possibly wish for in the world. When eleven of them had offered their gifts, the thirteenth suddenly entered the hall. She wanted to get revenge for not having been invited, and without greeting anyone or looking around, she cried out with a loud voice, "In her fifteenth year the princess shall prick herself with a spindle and fall down dead!"

That was all she said. Then she turned around and left the hall. Everyone was horrified, but the twelfth wise woman stepped forward. She still had her wish to make, and although she could not undo the evil spell, she could nevertheless soften it.

"The princess shall not die," she said. "Instead, she shall fall into a deep sleep for one hundred years."

Since the king wanted to guard his dear child against such a catastrophe, he issued an order that all spindles in his kingdom were to be burned. Meanwhile, the gifts of the wise women fulfilled their promise in every way: the girl was so beautiful, polite, kind, and sensible that whoever encountered her could not help but adore her.

Now, on the day she turned fifteen, it happened that the king and queen were not at home, and she was left completely alone in the palace. So she wandered all over the place and explored as many rooms and chambers as she pleased.

She eventually came to an old tower, climbed its narrow winding staircase, and came to a small door. A rusty key was stuck in the lock, and when she turned it, the door sprang open, and she saw an old woman in a little room sitting with a spindle and busily spinning flax.

"Good day, old granny," said the princess. "What are you doing there?"

"I'm spinning," said the old woman, and she nodded her head.

"What's the thing that's bobbing about in such a funny way?" asked the maiden, who took the spindle and wanted to spin too, but just as she touched the spindle, the magic spell began working, and she pricked her finger with it.

The very moment she felt the prick, she fell down on the bed that was standing there, and she was overcome by a deep sleep. This sleep soon spread throughout the entire palace. The king and queen had just returned home, and when they entered the hall, they fell asleep, as did all the people of their court. They were followed by the horses in the stable, the dogs in the courtyard, the pigeons on the roof, and the flies on the wall. Even the fire flickering in the hearth became quiet and fell asleep. The roast stopped sizzling, and the cook, who was just about to pull the kitchen boy's hair because he had done something wrong, let him go and fell asleep. Finally, the wind died down so that not a single leaf stirred on the trees outside the castle.

Soon a briar hedge began to grow all around the castle, and it grew higher each year. Eventually, it surrounded and covered the entire castle, so that it was no longer visible. Not even the flag on the roof could be seen. The princess became known by the name Beautiful Sleeping Briar Rose, and a tale about her began circulating throughout the country. From time to time princes came and tried to break through the hedge and get to the castle. However, this was impossible because the thorns clung together tightly as though they had hands, and the young men got stuck there. Indeed, they could not pry themselves loose and died miserable deaths.

After many, many years had gone by, a prince came to this country once more and heard an old man talking about the briar hedge. Supposedly there was a castle standing behind the hedge, and in the castle was a remarkably beautiful princess named Briar Rose, who had been sleeping for a hundred years, along with the king and queen and their entire court. The old man also knew from his grandfather that many princes had come and had tried to break through the briar hedge, but they had gotten stuck and had died wretched deaths.

"I am not afraid," said the young prince. "I intend to go and see the beautiful Briar Rose."

The good old man tried as best he could to dissuade him, but the prince would not heed his words.

Now the hundred years had just ended, and the day on which Briar Rose was to wake up again had arrived. When the prince approached the briar hedge, he found nothing but beautiful flowers that opened of their own accord, let him through, and then closed again like a hedge. In the castle courtyard he saw the horses and the spotted hunting dogs lying asleep. The pigeons were perched on the roof and had tucked their heads beneath their wings. When he entered the place, the flies were sleeping on the wall, the cook in the kitchen was still holding his hands as if he wanted to grab the kitchen boy, and the maid was sitting in front of the black chicken that she was about to pluck. As the prince continued walking, he saw the entire court lying asleep in the hall with the king and queen by the throne.

Then he moved on, and everything was so quiet that he could hear himself breathe.

Finally, he came to the tower and opened the door to the small room in which Briar Rose was asleep. There she lay, and her beauty was so marvelous that he could not take his eyes off her.

Then he leaned over and gave her a kiss, and when his lips touched hers, Briar Rose opened her eyes, woke up, and looked at him fondly.

After that they went downstairs together, and the king and queen woke up along with the entire court, and they all looked at each other in amazement. Soon the horses in the courtyard stood up and shook themselves. The hunting dogs jumped around and wagged their tales. The pigeons on the roof lifted their heads from under their wings, looked around, and flew off into the fields. The flies on the wall continued crawling. The fire in the kitchen flared up, flickered, and cooked the meat. The roast began to sizzle again, and the cook gave the kitchen boy such a box on the ear that he let out a cry, while the maid finished plucking the chicken.

The wedding of the prince with Briar Rose was celebrated in great splendor. And they lived happily to the end of their days.

JORINDE AND JORINGEL

III.

ONCE upon a time there was an old castle in the middle of a great, dense forest. An old woman lived there all by herself, and she was a powerful sorceress.

During the day she turned herself into a cat or a night owl, but in the evening she would return to her normal human form. She had the ability to lure game and birds, which she would seize and then cook or roast. If any man came within a hundred steps of the castle, she would cast a spell over him, so that he would not be able to move from the spot until she broke the spell.

If an innocent maiden came within her magic circle, she would change her into a bird and put her into a wicker basket. Then she would carry the basket up to a room in her castle where she had well over seven thousand baskets with rare birds of this kind.

Now, once there was a maiden named Jorinde, who was more beautiful than any other maiden in the kingdom. She was betrothed to a handsome youth named Joringel. During the time before their marriage, they took great pleasure in being in each other's company. One day they went for a walk in the forest so they could be alone and talk intimately with one another.

"Be careful," Joringel said, "that you don't go too close to the castle."

At dusk the sun shone brightly through the tree trunks and cast its light on the dark green of the forest. The turtledoves were singing mournfully in the old beech trees, and at times Jorinde wept. Then she sat down in the sunshine and sighed, and Joringel sighed too. They became very sad as if they were doomed to die, and when they looked around them, they became confused and did not know how to get home. The sun was still shining half above and half behind the mountains. When Joringel looked through the bushes and saw the wall of the old castle not very far away, he became so alarmed that he was nearly frightened to death, while Jorinde sang:

Oh, my bird, with your ring of red,
sitting and singing your tale of woe!
You tell us now that the poor dove is dead.
You sing your tale of woe – *oh-oh, oh-oh!*

Just then, as Joringel looked at Jorinde, she was turned into a nightingale singing *oh-oh, oh-oh!* A night owl with glowing eyes flew around her three times, and each time it cried, *"To-whoo! To-whoo! To-whoo!"*

Joringel could not budge. He stood there like a stone, unable to weep, to talk, or to move hand or foot. When the sun was about to set, the owl flew into a bush and then immediately returned as a haggard old woman, yellow and scrawny, with large red eyes and a crooked nose that almost touched her chin with its tip. She muttered something to herself, caught the nightingale, and carried it away in her hand. Joringel was still unable to speak, nor could he move from the spot. The nightingale was gone. Soon the woman came back and said with a muffled voice, "Greetings, Zachiel. When the moon shines into the basket, let him loose, Zachiel, just at the right moment."

Then Joringel was set free, and he fell on his knees before the woman and begged her to give Jorinde back to him, but she said he would never get her back again and went away. He shouted, he wept, he moaned, but it was all in vain. "Oh, no, what's to become of me?"

Joringel went off and eventually came to an unfamiliar village, where he tended sheep for a long time. He often went round and round the castle and always kept his distance. Finally, he dreamed one night that he had found a flower as red as blood, and in the middle of it was a pearl. He plucked the flower and went with it to the castle: everything that he touched with the flower was set free from the magic spell. He also dreamed that he managed to regain his Jorinde with the flower.

When he awoke the next morning, he began searching all over the mountains and valleys for the flower of his dream. He searched for nine days, and early on the ninth day he found a flower as red as blood. In its middle was a large dewdrop as big as the finest pearl. He carried this flower day and night until he reached the castle.

When he came to within a hundred steps of the castle, he was not spellbound but was able to get to the gate. Overjoyed by that, Joringel touched the gate with the flower, and it sprang open. So he entered, crossed the courtyard, and listened for the sound of birds. Finally, he heard them and went toward the room where the sorceress was feeding the birds in their seven thousand baskets. When she saw Joringel, she became angry, very angry. She began berating him and spitting poison and gall at him, but she could only come within two feet of him, and he paid no attention to her. Instead, he went and examined the baskets with the birds. Since there were hundreds of nightingales, he did not know how he would be able to find his Jorinde again. While he was examining the baskets, he noticed that the old woman had stealthily picked up one of the baskets and was heading toward the door.

Quick as a flash he ran over and touched the basket with the flower, and the old woman as well. Now she could no longer use her magic, and thus Jorinde appeared before him. She threw her arms around his neck and was just as beautiful as before. After Joringel had turned all the other birds into young women, he went home with his Jorinde, and they lived happily together for a long time.

THE BURIED TREASURE

Asked by students concerning the elusive goal, the quest of painting "out of the color," Gerard Wagner responded on one occasion by relating the gist of a Russian fairy tale – a version of which follows here.

Once upon a time, an old man lived in the Caucasus Mountains. He had a garden, and he worked in it all day long. He loved his garden very much.

His three sons loved the garden too. But they were lazy fellows and did not care for hard work. And hoeing, digging, planting, and carrying water is very hard work.

Still, each of the sons did do something now and then. The oldest went fishing. The middle son went hunting. And the youngest son took care of a neighbor's horses. But they did not bring much money home to their wives and children.

The years passed, and one day the father became too old to work. He called his sons to him and said, "Dear children, I will tell you a secret. I happen to know there is a treasure buried in my garden. You will inherit this garden after I die. If you keep digging in the earth, sooner or later you will find the treasure."

Not long after that the old man died. The sons grieved for their father. They buried him with great honor.

After a while they gathered their families, relatives, and friends together to discuss what should be done about the treasure.

"What if we have to dig up the entire garden before we find the treasure?" the oldest son said. "There is no way we can guess where it lies."

"Who knows how deep the treasure is buried? It will be such hard work," said the middle son.

The third son said, "What you say is true, yet how wonderful it would be to find this treasure. We would never have to work again!"

They started to dream aloud…

They would trade some of the gold they found for money and buy wonderful things, and when they ran out of money, there would always be enough gold to trade again. All day long they could sit cross-legged in a tavern, chatting with friends, drinking strong tea, and smoking long pipes. What a life it would be!

So they got down to work.

One morning while they were digging, their favorite uncle passed by. "Good day, my nephews," he said. "How is it coming along? I wish you good luck."

"It's hard going, dear Uncle," said the oldest. "And we certainly can use your good wishes. Who knows how long it will take us to find the treasure?"

"Indeed, who knows?" replied the uncle. "But since you are digging in the earth anyway, why don't you plant some seeds? Stop by my house and I will give you some."

The uncle gave the brothers plenty of seeds: pumpkin and melon seeds, cabbage and carrot seeds, parsley and pea seeds

And he gave them seeds for flowers: marigolds and morning glories, petunias and poppies, sweet williams and snapdragons.

And that was not all. He gave them saplings for apple, plum, apricot, and cherry trees, so that someday they could have an orchard.

The brothers did as their uncle had advised. They planted the seeds as they dug the soil. When they wanted to plant the saplings, they made especially deep holes. They watered the soil often.

Day after day, they worked under the hot sun. Their muscles grew stronger and their skin became so tanned that their teeth and the whites of their eyes sparkled like the snow on the Caucasian mountaintops. At noontime their wives brought them goat cheese, flat bread, sour milk, and cakes of rice and honey.

As time passed, the brothers began to love their work. They talked less and less about the treasure; often they forgot the reason they had started digging. The beautiful results of their months of labor began pushing and peeping through the earth.

At summer's end, the brothers had a fine harvest. They brought their vegetables and flowers to the market, and they were the best! Their watermelons were the reddest and ripest. How sweet were their Persian melons – and they had a wonderful aroma. And what flowers their wives sold! Wealthy women, even those from faraway mountain villages, came to buy them.

Year after year, the brothers worked hard in spring and summer, and in autumn they reaped a rich crop. When the villagers celebrated harvest time, the merriest parties were always held at the homes of the three brothers.

And so the three brothers realized how wise their father had been. They understood what their father had meant when he said that sooner or later they would find a treasure in the earth.

Selected Bibliography

Goethe, Johann Wolfgang von. *The Fairy Tale of the Green Snake and the Beautiful Lily*. Translated by Julius E. Heuscher. Edited by Joan deRis Allen. Paintings by Hermann Linde. Great Barrington, MA: SteinerBooks 2006.

Brothers Grimm. *The Complete Fairy Tales*. Translated, introduced, and annotated by Jack Zipes. Vintage Books, London 2007.

Stebbing, Peter. *Conversations about Painting with Rudolf Steiner. Recollections of Five Pioneers of the New Art Impulse*. Translated and edited by Peter Stebbing. Great Barrington, MA: SteinerBooks 2008.

Steiner, Rudolf. *Märchendichtungen im Lichte der Geistesforschung*. A public lecture held in Berlin, February 6, 1913. Contained in *Ergebnisse der Geistesforschung* (Results of Spiritual Research). CW 62. Rudolf Steiner Verlag, Dornach, Switzerland.

—— *Colour* (CW 291). Translated by John Salter and Pauline Wehrle. Sussex: Rudolf Steiner Press 1992.

Wagner-Koch, Elisabeth, and Wagner Gerard. *The Individuality of Colour. Contributions to a Methodical Schooling in Colour Experience*. With a Foreword by Sergei O. Prokofieff. Translated by Peter Stebbing. Rudolf Steiner Press 2009.

Wagner, Gerard. *Die Kunst der Farbe*. (The Art of Color). Contributions by E. Koch and K. Th. Willmann. Stuttgart: Verlag Freies Geistesleben 1980.

Wagner, Gerard (cont.)

—— *The Goetheanum Cupola Motifs of Rudolf Steiner / Paintings by Gerard Wagner.* With a Foreword by Sergei O. Prokofieff. Translated and edited by Peter Stebbing. Great Barrington, MA SteinerBooks 2011.

Portfolios

—— *Animal Metamorphosis*. Dornach, Switzerland. Philosophisch-Anthroposophischer Verlag 1972.

—— *Pflanzenmetamorphose* (Plant Metamorphosis). With an introduction by Elisabeth Koch. Philosophisch-Anthroposophischer Verlag, Dornach, Switzerland 1968. (Out of print).

—— *A Glance into Nature's Workshop*. An Artistic and Scientific Study. Introduction by E. Schuberth and G. Wagner. Philosophisch-Anthroposophischer Verlag am Goetheanum, Dornach, Switzerland 1974.

Exhibition Catalogues

—— The Hermitage, St. Petersburg 1997.

—— The Palace of Art, Cracow, Poland 2006.
(Both obtainable from the Goetheanum Bookshop, 4143 Dornach, Switzerland).

Woloschin, Margarita. *The Green Snake. Life Memories*. Translated by Peter Stebbing. Edinburgh, UK. Floris Books 2010.

Gerard Wagner in 1988
at work on murals in the dining hall of the Paracelsus Hospital, Unterlengenhardt, Germany

About Gerard Wagner

(1906–1999)

Gerard Wagner was born in Wiesbaden, Germany, April 5, 1906. He was two years old when his father died. A few years later he moved with his mother and two older brothers to England, where she had grown up. His schooling completed, he spent a year apprenticed to an Impressionist painter in the artists' colony of St. Ives in Cornwall, continuing his studies for a subsequent year at the Royal College of Art in London.

In 1926 he settled permanently in Dornach, Switzerland, where he became acquainted with the art impulse of Rudolf Steiner, studying with the painter Henni Geck. The rest of his life was dedicated to the elaboration of this new direction in art. Evolving a strict method of working, he sought to answer the fundamental question: *How does living form arise out of color?*

This requires gradually freeing oneself of mental images on the one hand, and of all unconscious arbitrariness on the other. Gerard Wagner especially developed the capacity to create metamorphoses on the same principle as Nature does, transposed to the sphere of art. In this way he found access to the realm of formative forces. His painting clearly sets itself apart from both naturalism and from the abstract art of the 20th century.

In working out Rudolf Steiner's indications, Gerard Wagner returned painting, the "art of color," to its spiritual origins.

Gerard Wagner's Fairy Tale Pictures

As timeless in feeling as Grimms' fairy tales themselves, the fairy tale pictures of Gerard Wagner were painted some fifty years ago. Besides *The Star-Taler*, *Briar Rose*, and *Jorinde and Joringel*, he also painted pictures for *Mother Holle* and *Rumpelstiltskin*. Especially aligned to children, not superficially but in their essential moral nature, and in accord with their own creative fantasy, Gerard Wagner's painting style during this period is characterized by forms that are clearly defined. Each series is individually attuned to the particular fairy tale mood. The present volume may be seen at the same time as an art book in its own right.

Gerard Wagner's subsequent work evolved further in the 1970s, 80s and 90s, (an example is shown here from 1993) and may be said to have developed to an unprecedented degree the possibilities of a living, mobile "etheric space" (as distinct from static, three-dimensional space). Here the art of painting especially takes on musical qualities. Wagner's work can be recognized as authentically modern.

The far-reaching prospect of a new art of painting in which form arises out of color was first demonstrated by Rudolf Steiner (1861–1925) in 1918 — in the paintings of the small cupola of the first Goetheanum in Dornach, Switzerland. Such a momentous new possibility in art remains little understood, and may still strike many people, artists included, as a "fairy tale" — as seemingly improbable. Epochal developments in art call for a reordering of sensibilities.

— *Peter Stebbing*

Gerard Wagner: *In Bethlehem*
(Plant Colors) 1993

About Peter Stebbing

Born in Copenhagen, Denmark, in 1941, Peter Stebbing attended Waldorf schools in England. Having studied at art schools in Brighton and London, he emigrated to the United States in 1966, continuing his studies at Cornell University and earning an M.F.A. degree in painting in 1968.

While teaching design and color courses over a period of six years at the City University of New York, he began a practical exploration of the scientific color phenomena set forth by Goethe in his color theory. This led eventually to a turning point — to the crucial question of finding a correspondingly lawful approach to color in painting.

The new and wholly different training in color experience begun in 1976 with the painter Gerard Wagner, on the basis of Rudolf Steiner's sketch motifs, resolved fundamental artistic questions with a coherent and systematic approach. Fully in accord with Goethe's discoveries and method, this approach may be termed "Goetheanistic."

Peter Stebbing subsequently established a painting school at the Threefold Educational Foundation in Spring Valley, NY., teaching there from 1983 until 1990. Since 1992 he has been director of the Arteum Painting School in Dornach, Switzerland (www.arteum-malschule.de.vu).

OTHER PUBLICATIONS TRANSLATED AND EDITED BY PETER STEBBING:

—— *The Rediscovery of Color* by Heinrich O. Proskauer. Anthroposophic Press 1986.

—— *EOS Art Journal,* Issues No. 1 (2007), No. 2 (2008), and No. 3 (2009).

—— *Conversations about Painting with Rudolf Steiner.* SteinerBooks 2008.

—— *The Individuality of Colour* by E. Wagner-Koch and G. Wagner. Rudolf Steiner Press 2009.

—— *The Green Snake /An Autobiography* by Margarita Woloschin. Floris Books 2010.

—— *The Goetheanum Cupola Motifs of Rudolf Steiner / Paintings by Gerard Wagner.* SteinerBooks 2011.